I0725976

The Sword and the River

Philip Baker

Published by

Dayglo Books Ltd, Nottingham, UK

www.dayglobooks.co.uk

0005-14-1602-13

Cover artwork & illustrations by
www.valentineart.co.uk

Typeset in Opendyslexic
by Abelardo Gonzales (2013)

Printed by IngramSpark

Distributed by Filament Publishing Ltd, Croydon

The Sword and the River

Chapter 1 – Glass in the River

I am a diver – an under-water explorer, you could say. Many years ago, I met up with friends and went diving in York, in the murky waters of the River Ouse.

There, almost under the Ouse Bridge, close to the centre of the ancient city, I was pleased to find a one-pint tankard made of dark green glass – such as I'd never seen before.

I brushed away a smear of mud – and with it went my joy. The 'green' was only a coating of slime on ordinary clear glass.

I surfaced. I was at 'The King's Staith'. This is an area of the riverside, now the beer garden of the King's Arms – an ancient public house. It often flooded.

Perhaps some visitors who didn't like the beer had found a handy way to get rid of it.

They threw it in the river, along with the very common clear glass tankard I had found.

Shortly afterwards, I made another dive in the same part of the river, but only found a couple of old glass bottles.

As I came out, I was approached by a man who had been watching me and my friends.

"What are you finding down there?" he asked, "anything interesting?"

I told him about the two glass tankards, but they didn't appear to interest him at all.

"Have you ever dived any further downstream? Anywhere between Acaster Malbis and Acaster Selby for example?"

We had not, and that seemed to disappoint him. Then he took me aside, saying he wanted a private word.

I had travelled alone that day. The other divers were in a hurry to get off home. That left me with my insistent questioner.

Chapter 2 – George's Sword

The man introduced himself as George. He led me to the King's Arms. We sat on the river bank, over-looking the water. George brought out drinks and started to tell me an astonishing story.

"I recently inherited a fine Viking sword," he began.

"It has a very vague history. It is said to have been found somewhere in, or near, this river, at Acaster Selby or very close to it.

"It is in remarkably good condition. I took it home and put it in a glass-topped display case. I thought that was the best place for it.

"That night I had a vivid dream of a Viking longship, with a high dragon's head at its bow. It was being rowed up a river. Its crew then landed, and set off inland.

"Unfortunately I was awakened by

a thunderstorm at that point.

"In the morning, when I looked at the sword, I had a feeling it was not quite as I'd left it. However, I didn't give it much thought.

"Two nights later, after I had examined the sword, I put it back in the display case.

"Its tip was towards the fireplace – as before. So it was pointing roughly south.

"That night my earlier dream was repeated. This time it lasted longer. I saw smoke rising from the direction the warriors had taken.

"In the morning I was alarmed to see the sword had turned as far as it could in the case.

"The tip was now pointing almost south-west.

"I put it back as I wanted it. Then I spent the rest of the day trying to find an explanation.

"I live alone. There were no visitors staying. I'm quite certain nobody could have come into the house and moved it."

I found my new friend's story baffling, but I wanted to hear more.

George told me that the following night his dream was repeated.

And so was the unexplained turning of the sword.

In a mixture of fear and bewilderment, George consulted a psychic.

Barbara, as she was called, professed to be able to interpret dreams.

Barbara's reaction was not entirely surprising. She thought the sword wanted to tell George something. She said it should be allowed freedom of movement.

So before going to bed that night, George removed the sword from the display case. He placed it centrally on the table's polished surface – pointing south.

"My dream was repeated," he related, "and it lasted even longer. This time the warriors returned to their ship, bearing loot. They were also dragging a couple of young women along with them.

"In the morning I found the sword pointed

due west, with its tip overhanging the edge of the table."

Clearly that old sword had a mind of its own.

George showed remarkable forethought. He used a compass to take the new bearing indicated by the sword. Then he returned it to its original position.

Two nights later the dream returned. The warriors were there, together with their loot and their captives. They boarded their ship and appeared about to sail away.

In the morning the sword had moved on to exactly the same compass bearing. Now it extended a full five inches beyond the edge of the table.

George consulted psychic Barbara again.

Chapter 3 – Compass bearings

Barbara remembered that George had taken compass bearings on the direction the sword was pointing in the morning.

She suggested they should do a test on the sword, using a compass.

"If compass bearings, from two different locations, are taken at the same time," Barbara pointed out, "the position of an object can be accurately plotted.

"My house is a full two miles south of yours. So why don't you come over, bring the sword with you, and sleep in my house for a couple of nights?"

George told me he was a little uncertain about that. He was not sure what her primary motive might be.

He was reassured when he learned that

Barbara was happily married. Her husband's name was Henry.

"I wasted no time accepting her invitation then," George told me.

"I took the sword to their house. I laid it, aligned south to north, on a suitable polished table.

"That night I dreamed of the arrival of a different, but bigger longship. The crew mounted a guard. Then the other warriors went marching off across country on another raid.

"Soon after, several men appeared who were very differently dressed.

"They attacked and slaughtered all three Vikings who had been left to guard the longship. And there my memory of the dream faded.

"But in the morning, the sword had turned on the table, and was pointing roughly north-west.

"Its bearing was checked by compass and recorded. Remarkably, the sword now overhung the table by almost half of its length."

There was much discussion between George, Barbara and her husband, Henry. They were mystified as to the significance of these events.

In George's dream, later that night, there was at first fog, out of which came Viking warriors, again with loot and several prisoners.

"But this time there was no longship to be seen," George told me.

"Only the dragon's head at its bow was left above the swiftly flowing waters. At the stern, just charred remains were visible.

"It was horrible. All the male prisoners were then axed, and their bodies thrown into the river. The Vikings and the women set off walking downstream, still burdened with their loot."

"In the morning my sword was found half off the table, indicating roughly westward.

"This time it also pointed downwards. The tip had come to rest deep in the upholstered arm of a chair beside the table."

Henry was a highways engineer. He had borrowed a six-inch-to-the-mile map from work.

On it they plotted the two compass bearings. These crossed a full hundred yards beyond the west bank of the River Ouse.

They were all surprised. They had expected the river itself to be the centre of interest.

Henry suggested that there need only be a slight error in the bearings to account for this.

In any case, the river could have changed its course over the flood plain during the thousand years since the sword was made.

Chapter 4 – The River Bank

That was George's long and improbable account of the recent past. Indeed, of the distant past, too – if his dreams were to be relied on.

But I was brought back to the present when he told me something else.

It appeared that Barbara's husband, Henry, was a water diviner – or dowser.

Henry wanted to test his skills out on the sword, on the riverbank. George invited me to come along next Sunday to see what would happen!

I didn't believe in water divining – I thought it was nonsense.

But I thought it might be an interesting experience to see what Henry did, so I accepted the invitation.

We met at Acaster Selby, and there I was introduced to the sword.

It was in remarkably fine condition.

Apparently it had been in the river for hundreds of years. It had reputedly been found somewhere between Acaster Malbin and Acaster Selby.

There are, in fact, almost three and a half miles of river between the two villages.

There was no suitable track, so we left the cars and made our way on foot along the river bank. We went towards the area indicated by the sword's strange behaviour.

As we walked together, Henry explained to me what he planned to do. I believe he sensed my doubt about his powers.

"I intend to carry the sword, point down," he explained. "First I'll try holding it by its cross-guard. I'll support the weight on my fingertips.

"If that becomes too tiring, I'll suspend it by a thin cord – like a pendulum – from a hazel rod. That's what we dowsers use for divining."

Henry began with the first method, and set off upstream. His starting point was well before the most southerly of the two bearing lines they had drawn on their map.

Henry asked us to keep clear, but I made sure I could see what he was doing because I felt his two-handed method was far too open to cheating.

George was with me, carrying a number of pointed wire rods with red or green tops.

Shortly after Henry passed the bearing line, he called, "Green!" As he moved on, George stuck the appropriate marker into the ground where Henry had been.

I had seen nothing, but twice in the next twenty or thirty yards Henry called "Green!"

At these times the blade did twitch slightly – towards the river.

Chapter 5 – The Red Marker

Ten yards further on and Henry cried, "RED!"

He kept walking, although his fingers must have been killing him by then.

There was one more "Green!" but nothing else until he had passed the northern bearing line.

Wearily, he passed the sword to me.

It was indeed a fearsome weapon. It was over a yard long, with a blade two and a half inches wide at the cross-guard.

I was greatly tempted to swing it around. I wanted to pretend to bring it down on the head of an imaginary foe – split him neatly into two halves.

But I thought such enthusiasm might not be fully appreciated, so I just admired it.

Henry produced a cord and tied it around

the top of the sword, then attached the other
end to the hazel rod.

On the return journey he stopped several
times to let the sword settle. I don't know what
he was expecting, but nothing happened.

Not, that is, until we neared the red marker.
There, I could detect some movement.

Henry stopped, steadied the sword and then
released it. Very slowly its tip swung towards
the river, slightly inclined downstream.

Three times he did this, the tip moving
a little further each time.

It was uncanny. There was no way he could
have faked that.

Five yards downstream – at the red marker
– he repeated the experiment.

The result was exactly the same, except
the tip now pointed at a right angle to the
riverbank.

Another five yards downstream, yet
another repetition, only this time the tip pointed
slightly upstream.

All this time, nobody had said a word.

It was as though we were afraid of breaking the spell. All I could hear were sharp intakes of breath. My own was amongst them.

Henry broke the silence – triumphantly.

"Back to the red marker!"

There he steadied the sword, released it, and the tip moved out towards the water.

Then, unbelievably, the sword began to rotate – only slowly at first – as though trying to screw itself into something.

Then in spun faster, until the cord suddenly snapped!

Although it only fell about a foot, the point of that ancient sword went at least three inches into the firm ground.

I could hardly believe what my eyes had just seen.

I would never believe that a fake sword – or even a skilfully crafted modern 'reproduction' sword – could behave like that. It must be truly ancient.

Chapter 6 – Leadership Qualities

"Now you know where you'll have to dive!"

George was in his element. He was clearly intent on taking charge.

But I, and my friends, would be the ones doing any diving. George knew nothing about the difficulties and dangers that would involve.

From experience, I knew that there was little chance of any ship's timbers surviving in flowing water for almost a thousand years.

However, I thought, . . . just perhaps . . . Some parts of the ship may have been buried by mud, very soon after it sank. In that case, who knows what might still be preserved down there?

We would need help to investigate further but we also needed to be discrete. George offered to take the lead in contacting people.

I wasn't happy about that. I thought he was too excitable and would talk too much.

I managed to persuade George to let Henry make enquiries on our behalf. Henry worked for the Council, so he had some useful contacts.

Henry did some valuable research. He was able to confirm that there had been no river straightening done. Nor had any dredging been done in that area.

He had also learned that almost a hundred years ago a very fine, and undoubtedly original Viking sword was recovered from the River Ouse.

It had been found close to a place that had once been a Viking chief's stronghold. It was known as Cawood castle.

Cawood was little more than two miles downstream from where we were going to dive to search the river bed.

Henry had also found out when the tidal flow would be at its weakest. This was of great interest. Diving around that time ought to make our search a little easier.

I arrived the next weekend, with two fellow divers, friends of mine named Peter and Jack.

There was no convenient road, or even a track for the cars. I had to organise all hands to carry our equipment to the 'red' area.

I took a wicked pleasure in loading George up heavily. I thought it would help him show off his leadership qualities.

Chapter 7 – Nil Visibility

The three of us divers kitted up. Peter and I would go in first, with Jack to act as standby diver.

We agreed to enter the water some eighty yards upstream of the red marker, where the sword had shown no interest. Then we would make our way slowly downstream.

Because of the need to explore the bottom by touch, we went in heavily weighted. Under the water we set off, feeling our way as we went.

I expected poor, or even nil visibility. I was relying on the current to carry away any mud we might disturb.

In fact the whole operation reminded me of how some Second World War divers worked. The difference was they were feeling for mines and other explosive devices that were booby-trapped.

By contrast, we were seeking a possibly vanished, and certainly harmless old sunken boat.

I took the bank side. Peter and I were fastened together by a line. It was just long enough to allow us to touch fingertips. It prevented Peter from straying further towards the middle of the river.

My weights were just right. I moved along half-crawling. Both my hands were sliding over the mud as I worked with them.

My left hand was crossing to and fro over the bottom, in front of me. Meanwhile, my right hand was searching up the curve of the bank.

I had also taken down some 'spears'. These were steel rods, three feet long, sharply pointed at one end. They were bent round and welded into a handle at the other end. I could use these to probe into the mud.

Down there in the murky depths, it was difficult for Peter and I to be sure of our exact location.

I had told Jack, my standby, to throw a small banger onto the water when he saw our bubbles some five yards from the red marker.

On hearing the bang I began to use one of my 'spears'. I probed into the mud. I was hoping to find wood, but without any luck.

My spear went almost two feet into the river bottom. Nowhere did it meet any definite resistance.

Peter had had no better luck with either hands or spear.

Then, at one point, further downstream of the red marker, I encountered what I believed was a large stone. It was buried some twelve inches down in the mud.

I surfaced.

Chapter 8 – Making Some Money

I asked the shore party to record my position.

To be honest, this was rather more to show them that I was doing my job. I didn't really believe I'd made a significant discovery.

From what I'd learned about other river finds, wood lying under less than two feet of mud could have been preserved to some degree.

In several cases wood dating from Roman times had been found.

This had been at sites where it was known there had been a bridge. The Roman timbers were the remains of bridge supports driven into the river bed.

It was worth our while to keep on looking, so I went down once more.

Before I gave the signal to surface again, my hand closed around a familiar shape.

It was an old-fashioned, pointed-bottomed mineral-water bottle. There were others with it, so we'd not go home empty-handed!

I tugged on the line connecting me to Peter. I took his hand and guided it down to show him what I had found.

Then he started looking around as well. We surfaced with two bottles apiece. We threw them up on to the bank and went down for more.

In all, we brought out fifteen glass bottles. Four of them had marble stoppers. They were unusual.

We found a couple of stoneware ginger beer containers, too.

A nice collection – five different types of Victorian and Edwardian bottles.

Peter and I knew a small-time antique dealer who would be interested, especially in any bottle with a marble stopper.

Our discovery meant that, to some small

degree, our expenses for the day would be covered. That was no bad thing.

George had made no suggestion about paying us.

He probably believed he had been generous enough in allowing us to share in his great discovery and fame – if that is what it should turn out to be.

Finding so many bottles suggested we were close to what had once been a favourite picnic spot. Or, more likely, a safe mooring place for boats.

The river had rolled these discarded bottles into a hollow. The swift, eddying current had kept them free of mud.

Chapter 9 – The Spinning Sword

I would never have believed an inanimate object could behave the way that sword had done.

I had no explanation, but I felt our only hope now lay with the weapon itself.

I had access to an inflatable dinghy. It was agreed that we would bring this to the river.

Henry would come aboard the dinghy with the sword. As we progressed along the water we would see what – if anything – it would tell us.

Secretly I was worried that the sword might decide to throw a real wobbly. If it did, we could end up capsized, or punctured.

And what would George say to me if his sword went back into the river, and was never recovered?

The inflatable dinghy had an outboard motor. We discussed using this but in the end we decided to leave it behind.

We were worried that its coils and other electrics might interfere with the sword, and Henry's dowsing powers.

Without the motor, that meant rowing. But rowing was out of the question because the current was too strong. We needed power of some sort.

Henry, as always, knew the right person. He managed to borrow a motorboat with a very long tow rope.

Henry and I were to be in the dinghy, with the motorboat up ahead towing us.

Henry would sit in the bows with the sword hanging from the hazel rod.

I would sit at the stern. As soon the sword went into action, I would drop a concrete weight overboard with a marker buoy to fix the exact spot.

I had first planned to bring a cast iron

weight, but then remembered it would be much better to use a non-metallic one.

On the day, everything went as planned. The motorboat was waiting for us with a driver.

George invited himself on board the motorboat, which kept him out of our way.

Henry and I got into the inflatable dinghy. We set off, the motorboat towing us steadily along.

At first, in midstream, the sword sulked, hanging motionless.

As we drew closer to the red marker the sword slowly began to swing, getting faster and faster.

When we neared the bank, the tip began circling.

Further out, the circling slowed down. When we moved upstream and then downstream it also slowed the circling.

The critical position was plotted from the shore. It was some ten feet out from the bank, and almost opposite the red marker.

When we stopped there, the sword began to spin on its cord, faster and faster.

I shouted to Henry to stop it, before it could break free and bore a hole through the bottom of the boat!

At the same time I made certain we should know the exact position by dropping my weight overboard with the marker buoy attached.

Chapter 10 – The Magnet-o-meter

Only when we were back ashore did I reveal the contents of a large wooden box I had brought with me.

It was a state-of-the-art, underwater metal detector called a Magnet-o-meter.

Using all my charm, I had managed to persuade the manufacturers to lend it to us. I promised them they would get free publicity if we could recover what we hoped their gadget would locate.

Being mysterious and secretive with the manufacturers had been easy enough, because I had no real idea what it was we were looking for.

I was not even sure if it had ever been made with any kind of metal in it, or if any metal would still be left.

Only the sword knew that — and it certainly wasn't sharing any of its secrets with me.

As a test, I went into the water and moved around on the bottom, close to the bank, holding the Magnet-o-meter out in front of me until I heard it bleep.

And there below it was the large steel nut and bolt I'd thrown in a few minutes earlier. So far so good.

I repeated the exercise and found the nut alone. Better, but what about the very thin steel washer? Yes, even that registered at about a couple of feet.

So far very good, but would the Magnet-o-meter be able to penetrate mud?

I had come well prepared to find out. Those on shore passed me a length of rod on which was a nut, similar to the one just detected.

I thrust it some 18 inches down into the mud, and still got a healthy bleep.

Next, I reversed the rod, pushing a washer about as deep, and still got a passable signal.

By now, I was beginning to have real faith in the Magnet-o-meter.

I made my way out from the bank to where the current was stronger and would make things rather more difficult. Then I moved down the buoy line to the weight at the bottom.

Holding on to the weight, with the Magnet-o-meter held at both arms' length, I passed it around the weight in a circle with a radius of almost five feet. Nothing happened.

Could it be the sword was leading us on a merry dance? Or did it have powers beyond those of present-day technology?

I tried another full circle only three feet from the weight, and downstream there was just the hint of a bleep.

The closer to the weight, the more distinct the bleep.

I knew there was no metal in that lump of concrete. I had been tempted to attach a ring for the rope to go through but hadn't done so.

To be sure, I needed to move the weight.

I managed to reposition it a yard upstream. That wasn't easy because it was pushing me down into the mud as I tried to move it. It was so heavy.

But now there was no doubt. The Magnet-o-meter was telling me that something metal was lying almost where the weight had been.

Magnet-o-meter and the sword seemed to agree with each other on that.

But what was it down there? And how deep?

Time to go ashore to give the good news, and to consult with the others.

Chapter 11 – The Spirit of the Vikings

"The best bleep came from where we dropped the weight," I told them. "But it won't be easy to estimate the size of the object."

"Why is that?" George asked.

"You remember, when I was testing, a small washer registered under almost two feet of mud.

"But a larger object, lying deeper, would give a similar signal. So would a very large one even deeper still. So we can't be sure how big this object is unless we can dig it out and have a look at it.

"And," I pointed out, "the mud there is very soft. It won't be easy to dig in."

"But if it's so soft, surely it must be easy to dig." George was – as always – talking faster than he was thinking.

"It doesn't work like that," I explained. "As I dig some mud out, more will slide in. We've got to do some deep thinking about this – and possibly some deep digging, too!"

Forethought was definitely needed.

We could have another go with our spears, though perhaps better not to. Probing like that could easily damage whatever was down there.

That meant exploring by hand.

I hadn't yet tried forcing my hand down into the mud. I just had to hope, when I did, I didn't find anything sharp down there.

"Jack," I told my standby, "you'd better come in, too – just in case I get stuck, or get dragged down by the Spirit of the Vikings, or whatever may be lurking down there!"

In fact, when I went back underwater and tried, I could only get my fingers about six inches into the mud.

So it would have to be digging.

And before digging could start, we need a plan of action.

I felt it was important that our activities should remain secret, so I insisted that the buoy marking the spot should be removed.

We brought it to the shore and hid it underwater at the bank side. We weighted its rope down to the bottom. With luck, boat traffic would not be inconvenienced.

I asked Henry to contact the River Authority to find our whether they had any objections to a small excavation at the centre of the river bed.

I told him to emphasise 'centre'. We needed to assure them there would be no danger of us undermining the banks.

Then it was time to go home and begin some serious thinking.

Chapter 12 – The Coffer Dam

Back at home, I spent a lot of time working out how best to set about digging a hole underwater.

Many of my best ideas come to me when I'm soaking in the bath. This one was no exception.

I would need a portable wall – or what is called a 'coffer-dam' – around me under the water. This would prevent mud slipping into the hole.

But what size coffer-dam? I stood up and started imaginary digging.

Yes, I could work within the overall dimensions of my bathtub – two feet by five feet – and with a maximum height of two feet.

The next question was what materials my coffer-dam should be made of?

It would surely be advisable to avoid any metal, because of using the Magnet-o-meter.

So . . . plywood. Special marine plywood is glued, avoiding the use of metal nails or screws. The extra expense would be justified.

The coffer-dam would be positioned on the river bed. I would dig standing inside it.

With careful use of the spade, I could sink the coffer-dam down deeper as I dug the mud away.

To add height, if necessary, a duplicate coffer-dam could be added on top.

Easily said, but less easily done underwater. As the mud was stirred up by my digging, visibility would soon be reduced to nil.

But, 'Nothing ventured, nothing gained,' I thought to myself.

I set about making a scale model of a coffer-dam.

After I'd finished, I decided to alter the 'bathtub' dimensions of my original plan a little. My coffer-dam was 6 feet long and 2 feet wide.

The sides and ends would be hinged together using stout canvas. The canvas would be glued on the insides of two diagonally opposite corners, and on the outside of the other two corners.

This would allow the whole thing to fold flat so it was easy to transport.

All good archaeologists think in terms of 'trenches' and how deep they should be dug.

I settled for a depth of eighteen inches for my coffer-dam, which would be like an artificial trench.

The natural buoyancy of the plywood could become a problem. Lead weights to keep it down were the obvious answer, but would lead register on the metal detector? I couldn't risk it.

So it had to be concrete weights, with rope handles – for convenience – and four pegs on the underside to straddle the corners.

Two additional coffer-dams were made on the same principle. These were shallower – only six inches deep. They could be fitted on top of the first one, to build up the depth, if necessary.

They had strips of plywood glued to the middle of each part, to slide outside the first coffer-dam, to keep them fastened together.

It worked well enough on land, but . . . underwater? Only time would tell.

There was one more thing I needed. I approached the local archaeological society. They put me in touch with a maker of fine mesh screens, or 'riddles' as some folk like to call them.

They were horribly expensive, but essential. All the mud we dug up would be sieved in the riddle. We didn't want to lose anything that was buried in it.

Then we were ready to go in search of whatever it might be that the sword and the Magnet-o-meter agreed was so interesting.

Chapter 13 – Trophies in the Water

The completed coffer-dam was eight-foot-long when it was folded flat. Peter and Jack and I struggled with it.

We rehearsed on dry land before taking it to the river. When we lowered it into the water we managed to get it weighted into position without too much difficulty.

We put it in line with the flow of the river.

I started to dig, using a trowel. I decided a spade was too insensitive a tool. Peter and Jack worked the riddle, sieving the mud that I dug up.

I soon found that the coffer-dam would sink down satisfactorily if I worked all round its base.

Jack tugged my arm and held up two similar shaped small pieces of rusty metal. These came from only few inches down in the mud.

I used the detector again, to check whether there was more metal down there.

Yes, there most definitely was, but – sod's law – it, whatever it may be, lay right at the east side of the coffer-dam, and could quite possibly extend beyond it.

My digging had reduced visibility to almost nil inside the coffer-dam.

Outside the coffer-dam the current cleared the riddle almost at once, which was how Jack had spotted the two objects.

It was time to surface with our trophies. Anyway, we needed a rest before adding the next layer of the coffer-dam.

Luckily Henry recognised what we had found. They were, he told us, a pair of 'ox cues'. These were similar to horseshoes, but nailed to the hooves of working oxen, rather than horses.

Henry didn't know whether the Vikings used to use these, but he was fairly certain the Vikings didn't bring any oxen with them. So they were probably not a significant find, although quite interesting to see.

Back in the water again, I resisted the temptation to dig straight down to reach the metal. I worked steadily, trying to take the whole trench down a couple of inches at a time.

And then, almost two feet down, on the west side, I found wood. It was firm, though a bit spongy. I felt fairly sure it was hand-worked, not natural tree wood.

This was wonderful news, but it meant that the coffer-dam could only go down to that level.

I grabbed Pete's hand and made him touch my find, and he did the same to Jack. Then we solemnly shook hands. It was exciting to think that we three were the only ones who knew it was there.

For the next few minutes I revelled in the knowledge that I was the first person to touch that timber in very, very many years.

Even more carefully now, I dug on. Little by little, I continued to lower the whole surface of the mud inside the coffer-dam.

I realised the surface of the wood I had found sloped into the trench. I could even feel the joint where one plank overlapped another. But there was nothing caught by the riddle, so I carefully carried on.

Then I touched what could only be a curved piece of timber, like the rib of a boat. It was lying at right angles against the planks. Yes! It must surely be that we have indeed found a boat!

But how long had it been down there? Was it hundreds of years – or merely tens of years? If only the visibility was better . . .

I was almost out of air when my trowel touched something hard, where the detector told me there was metal.

It didn't feel like stone, and I worked my fingers into the mud to explore further. It was smooth, and rounded. I pulled gently and it came away. I held it up into clearer water. It was metal – beyond a doubt . . .

But one glance at my gauge told me I had almost no air left. I thumped Pete on the shoulder and signalled to him that I was going up.

Pete and Jack followed my example, not knowing what tale I had to tell.

Chapter 14 – Our Treasure

Ashore, I kept my find behind my back.

I tried to keep it hidden whilst telling the others about the boat. I described the boat as best I could using only one hand.

Then, holding out my find, I asked: "And what do you think THIS is?"

I was sharing my own first proper sight of it with them.

Lying on my palm, it was almost six inches in diameter, flat, then becoming domed at the centre.

I guessed it was made of brass or something similar.

It had six small holes equally spaced around the edge. These had once held iron nails or rivets. They had almost entirely rusted away.

There was much discussion as to what it could be. Then I spotted there was a shallow groove across it.

"See that cut? Could it have been made with a sword, perhaps?

"This must be from a shield. It's probably the central boss. And – if I am right – there must surely be other bits down there, too!"

It was such an exciting prospect!

"We are going to be famous!"

I got quite carried away with myself for a minute, but common sense reasserted itself.

"Don't you think the time has come to get one of the York museums involved?

"And somehow we must try to make sure nobody else dives here, and steals OUR treasure."

Chapter 15 – Cause and Effect

There was general agreement about the need to involve a museum.

But which one? And who should do the approaching?

My difficulty was going to be keeping certain people out of the museum – namely George and his psychic friend Barbara, and her husband Henry with his dowsing skills.

I felt certain we would very quickly be shown the door. No serious museum curator or archaeologist would believe our story about the strange behaviour of the sword that had started it all.

My suggestion was as tactful as possible.

"Perhaps, as the actual finder of the shield boss – if that is what it is – I might be the best person to get things started."

My thinking was, that after asking for secrecy about the find, I would tell the museum only that we had dived somewhere between Acaster Malbis and Acaster Selby.

Not surprisingly, George wanted to be in from the start, but Henry managed to persuade him that I was right.

And so it was agreed, and we all shook hands on it.

I would give no hint to the museum that we had an unconventional – but very good reason – to dive where we did. I'd explain that I had found both the shield boss, and parts of a boat.

Only when, and if, the museum showed real interest, would I say more. Otherwise, I would not mention the extraordinary – indeed, quite incredible – circumstances that had led us to excavate there and so make the discovery.

In other words, first tell the believable effect, and only afterwards explain the almost unbelievable cause!

Chapter 16 – A Visit to the Museum

I visited several museums to see which was the most willing to deal with the public.

I found the name of the top man at the Aldwark Museum. It was Roger Atkinson. I asked for a private interview with him.

I said we had made what we believed was an important discovery. I could bring part of my find with me. I insisted that my visit, and my find, must be treated as secret for a short time.

I sensed a reluctance, so I promised that if he was not interested, I could be in and out of his office in less than five minutes.

In fact my visit to Mr Atkinson lasted almost an hour. The museum's Viking specialist, James Burton, joined us.

He gladly confirmed my identification of the shield boss. He explained that it was not only decorative, but functional, covering a hole in the shield.

A wooden bar was attached to the back of the shield, which the warrior would grip. His knuckles would protrude through the hole. The dome of the boss protected them – as proved by the deep cut in the metal.

However, the specialist was much more interested in the boat.

I described what I had felt, but not seen, down there. Then I cautiously started to tell them about George's sword – of which they knew nothing at all, of course.

The more I told them about its weird behaviour, the more sceptical they became.

I pointed out that I only dived in that stretch of the river because of what it had told us.

"I only dug down in that spot, because the sword, and the Magnet-o-meter, agreed," I told them.

"And that is where the boat, and if we are

lucky, any other parts of the shield's metalwork still lie."

Both of them looked distinctly unhappy.

Mr Atkinson, the curator, spoke first.

"If it were not for what you've just shown us . . . I'd have to be thoroughly professional and say I cannot believe a single word of what you have told us.

"As it is, we'll be risking our reputations by even giving you a little of our time, let alone any help. But . . . the potential is enormous.

"Even a few planks from a Viking longship – if that is indeed what you have found – that would be wonderful! And who knows what else?"

I reminded him about the need for secrecy.

"Of course we will keep it under wraps," Mr Atkinson agreed.

"We must make sure the press don't get hold of your story of how the sword led you there. Just imagine the utter nonsense they would make of that!

"Do you think you can get your people to

keep their tongues under control?" he asked.

"I do have to say I'm worried about George," I confessed. "Do you think it might be possible to get him in here? Say you would very much like to see his sword.

"Then, perhaps treat him as if he is very important. But also threaten no help at all will be forthcoming if any part of the story leaks out. A sort of carrot and big stick approach?"

"Yes. I can be very stern if need be – or so my kids tell me," Mr Atkinson smiled.

"And I need a cover story, too," I added.

"Why did I dive there? I suppose I could say I was told about an outboard motor being lost in the river, and being a helpful sort of chap, I said I'd take some friends and look for it. No need to mention I was digging deep in the mud when I made my discoveries."

"That sounds plausible enough, even sensible," Mr Atkinson agreed.

He was serious, indeed almost worried.

"There is the problem of how to protect

your site. Somebody must have seen what you were doing.

"If you were diving in the sea, on an ancient wreck, there would be the Protection of Wrecks Act that has just come into effect. But you are a very long way from the sea."

"Yes." I agreed, "but we are still in tidal waters. I can only leave this problem in your hands, but the sooner there is legal control of the site the better."

There was general agreement because we all felt that the discovery – and whatever was in the water – was far too important to be left unprotected.

Chapter 17 – Carry On Diving!

"My immediate question is," I continued, "do you want me to dive some more?"

"Yes! Please do carry on diving. But it is most important that you record exactly where you find anything."

"I had no time to use the Magnet-o-meter after I got hold of the shield boss," I explained, "so I don't know if there's any more metal down there."

"I know that will be difficult," Mr Atkinson stressed, "but it is essential that we – you – do treat this as an archaeological excavation. It's not just simple treasure hunting."

"Understood." I nodded agreement.

"I think, for the moment, you should go as deep as you can in your present trench – we'd better call it 'trench one'.

"That won't be a problem. Our coffer-dams are still down there . . . slowly filling up with mud."

"Very good. Use those, but don't start anything new."

"Okay."

"Do you know whether the planks are straight, or curved? Curves would indicate you are at one end of the boat."

"So far as I could tell, the planks – what little I've uncovered – are straight."

"What we do need, most of all, is detailed measurements. Not only the size of the individual timbers, but the shape of the hull itself."

"That will be very difficult. Photography will be impossible. Lights are useless down there because of the particles in the water . . . like using headlights in dense fog."

"There must be a way you could do it."

I cast around in my mind. I remembered that in the school physics lab we had stands with special clamps. You could fix a rod at any height and at a right angle – height and angle both being readily adjustable.

Perhaps I could devise something like that. I would have to find a way of keeping it vertical and fixed as a reference point. Then, it should be possible to extend other rods sideways, out to the timbers.

That way, I could get at least a crude idea of the shape of the hull.

I quickly explained my idea to the museum people.

"Do you have the resources to get a gadget like that made?" I asked. "Remember, I'll be working almost entirely by touch."

"I'll have a big think about it." The Viking specialist sounded enthusiastic. "Something like you describe could work."

"I know a man who runs a small engineering business," Mr Atkinson interrupted. "As it happens, he's a keen amateur archaeologist.

"If I ask him, I'm sure he'll be only too willing to build us something. A device based on clamps and rods could solve the problem of measuring under water."

"Sounds good to me."

"The first problem will be keeping the upright vertical." The Viking specialist was into his stride now.

I had foreseen that difficulty myself. I was glad to see he and I were thinking along the same lines.

"If you do manage it," the Viking specialist continued, "ideally, you will need to record each plank just above the overlap. That way we'd get a true profile."

I could see he was getting excited at the prospect.

"Please," he implored me, "as soon as you can, let me have very rough measurements.

"I will," I told him.

"I'd like the width of the planks and the depth of wood you can see, or have exposed."

I promised him I would do my best.

"And . . ."

I wondered why I wasn't surprised there was more.

". . . it would be very difficult, but could you possibly make some sort of sketch of the shape of the boat?

"Could you do a view of it, as seen from the bow or stern?"

All I could do was promise him I would try.

"How big is this coffer-dam of yours?" Mr Atkinson asked.

"Six feet by two feet."

"Did you did say it lies roughly along the side of the boat?"

Rather than more lengthy explanations, I drew him a rough sketch.

"Next time we meet," he assured me, "we'll have a working version of your idea, and you can tell me if you can handle it under the water.

"We'll try to imagine using it in the dark – which is as near as I'll ever get to doing what you do."

I thanked him and we shook hands.

"I think," the Viking specialist added before I left, "seeing as we'll be working together a lot, it would be better if you call me Jim."

I was intrigued to know what the museum would come up with. I hoped I wouldn't have to wait too long to find out.

Chapter 18 – The Measuring Device

The next time I dived, I took the Magnet-o-meter down with me and got an immediate, encouraging bleep.

It soon became clear that this came from two separate sources, perhaps thirty inches apart.

Both were close to the side of the coffer-dam, and aligned with the planks of the boat.

Resisting temptation to get going with a shovel, I carefully worked the whole surface down almost three inches, but found nothing.

Then my trowel was scraping on metal. Time to start digging with my fingers instead.

Before I began, I carefully memorised the position of the objects. Feeling carefully around them, I found nothing else connected. I first eased one, then the other free of the mud.

I moved into clearer water, and there
I saw two pieces of intricately decorated brass,
or possibly bronze. They were both studded with
small, dark red stones. I later learned these
were garnets.

It took me a little while to work out that
these must be decorations on the top and
bottom of a sword's scabbard.

No wonder George's sword had been so
excited! Surely it was because it would soon be
reunited with its old companions.

Understandably, there was much
excitement on shore, too, when I showed off my
latest discoveries.

I was due at the Aldwark Museum the next
day. I decided to have a little fun there, so
I kept my carefully wrapped finds in my pocket.

I was genuinely alarmed by what Jim Burton,
the Viking specialist, showed me.

It was a heavy metal bar, turned over into
a hook at the top. At regular intervals below,
there were lengths of thin tube welded on at
right angles.

Each had a nut welded on the outside, with a bolt screwed into it. Through each tube was a length of close-fitting steel rod.

Jim explained it to me.

"This is how we think it can work. And of course, we can make it bigger or cut some off, or weld on anything else you need.

It looked complicated enough already to me. I didn't like the idea of welding on anything else.

"You will need a suitable length of wood across the coffer-dam," Jim continued. "Hang the hook over that – with all the rods central, so as to balance the weight. Then it should hang vertically.

"We'll fit a rod to the back. You can extend that to the bottom of your trench. It will keep the whole thing vertical. We've yet to do that.

"When this device is fixed in place, the idea is that you extend the rods, one at a time, out to the timber.

"When the first rod touches the timber, you screw the bolts home to lock the rod in place.

"Do you follow me?"

"Yes, Jim, I do."

"Good. You repeat that with each rod in turn until they are all extended and locked off.

"That way, when you bring the whole contraption up with you, the measurements from each rod will be preserved. Any comments?"

I admired the ingenuity that had gone into producing the measuring gadget.

"Looks good to me, Jim. Just one question. How do I tighten up the bolts? It will be difficult to use a spanner down there."

"Yes. I found it difficult in the dark, feeling every time I needed to use the spanner. I was trying to do it with an open-ended one. But Bill, our engineering friend, has made this for you."

He produced a box spanner. It had an open-mouthed cone welded on one end and a T-piece on the other.

"Use this to guide the spanner onto the head of the bolt, and then twist hard."

He demonstrated and it worked perfectly.

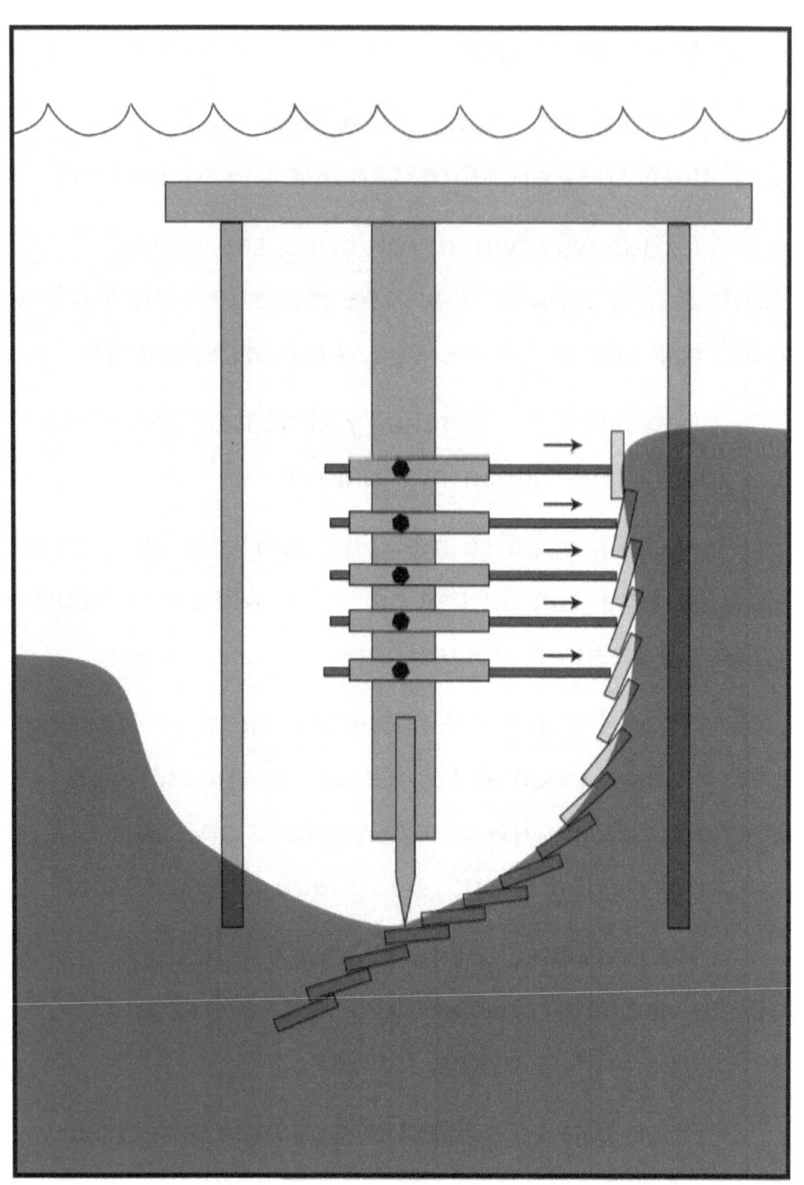

"That rod down the back," I said, "it had better be pointed, so that I can drive it into the wood – not far, just enough to make sure the measurements are accurate."

"No problem, but only as far as is absolutely necessary. One day that boat might go on show, and we don't want people seeing that you left your mark there."

I laughed. It was a temptation to 'leave my mark'.

Chapter 19 – Left Behind by the Vikings

"On a more general topic," Jim continued, "did you know that the ancient records tell us that the Viking King Harald needed 300 ships to carry his men here?

"They landed near York in 1066. After their defeat at the Battle of Stamford Bridge, only 24 ships were needed to carry the survivors back to Norway?"

"I know about the battle," I replied, "but I didn't know about all those ships. Are you suggesting we have found one of the 276 ships that were left behind?"

"Well, it's a line of reasoning . . . of possibility . . .

"Though how and why it got from where it landed to where you found it is for your lot to decide."

I reached into my pocket.

"But, Jim," I said, "those ships were not the only things the Vikings abandoned. How about these little beauties?"

I handed him the plastic bag with its wet contents.

When he unwrapped the bronze and garnet ornaments, his surprise, and satisfaction, were more than evident.

"These are superb workmanship. They could only have belonged to an important man.

"Where did you find them? And do you know what they are?"

I explained as best I could where I had discovered them.

Jim marked their positions on the crude plan he was making of our underwater excavations.

Chapter 20 – Another Trophy

When Peter, Jack and I dived again the next weekend, we found quite a lot of silt had built up in the coffer-dam.

It was rather more than I had expected. At least this explained how quickly the boat could have filled up with mud when it first sank.

The mud would have helped to preserve the inner side of the timbers of the boat.

What the outside would be like I had yet to discover.

My first task was to do a further search with the Magnet-o-meter. I got a good result.

Again, at the very edge of the coffer-dam – close to where I'd removed the shield boss – there was a loud bleep.

The new mud was easy to get rid of.

It was so soft it was almost liquid, and tended to flow off my trowel.

When I reached the undisturbed level, another check with the Magnet-o-meter gave an even louder bleep, but in the same place.

I dug down carefully with the trowel and felt something hard.

Then I remembered what Jim had said about recording. I measured with my fingers along the wood. It was exactly three spans from the end of the coffer-dam.

I then worked my hand into the mud and found – so far as I could tell – metal.

Because I could see nothing through the muddy water, I closed my eyes to concentrate on my touch.

The object was a thin wedge shape, tapering to nothing.

I soon realised it could be an axe.

I felt along its upper edge, and then the cutting edge.

I followed on round the sharp angle.

My fingers curved back towards the hole where the wooden shaft would have been.

And to my surprise, there it was – still smooth and rounded.

That was both good and bad news. The shaft could be at least a yard in length.

It pointed diagonally along my trench, but might well continue under the mud on the opposite side.

How fortunate it was that I'd not just pulled up the axe head. I would probably have broken the shaft in the process.

I continued digging deeper. It was now more awkward to pass the unwanted mud over the coffer-dam wall into Peter's riddle.

It occurred to me that it would only be possible to test out the measuring device once enough mud had been cleared.

Whenever my trowel began to scrape on wood, I had to be much more careful.

I kept on thinking there ought to be a way of swilling out the last of the mud.

I ran my fingers along the axe shaft. I needed to know where not to dig. But after about eight or so inches, it ended.

Could it be that it had been broken all those years ago?

Anyhow, it would now come out more easily.

And we'd have another trophy (though perhaps it would better not to use that word when I took it to the Aldwark Museum).

Chapter 21 – Dating Our Finds

Fortunately, my air lasted long enough for me to complete the excavation of the axe. Some some ten inches of its shaft remained. It had broken by splitting lengthways rather than snapping across squarely.

Back at the Aldwark Museum, Jim Burton was disappointed that I'd not used the measuring device.

However, he was delighted with the axe, and that I had kept it wet all the way back to the museum.

"It's a bearded axe," he explained. "They usually had a quite a short shaft. It's a well-known type, so that will help a little with dating. Useful as a tool, and as a weapon, too.

"But look here, at the underside of the shaft, at the top of the break – there's a cut."

I looked, and it was clear to see.

"That's why it broke," Jim explained, "when it struck home into something – or perhaps somebody. I wonder if that was done with a sword . . ."

"Like the cut on the shield boss?" I wondered.

Jim nodded. Then he changed the subject.

"I think I know how you can get accurate measurements of the planks for me."

"Oh, yes. How is that?"

"I've got some modelling clay. If you mould that into a thin sheet and press the edge against the wood, you should bring back a good impression of one plank and its two neighbours."

It would be the first time I'd ever tried working with modelling clay underwater. I could see how useful it would be, if I could manage to do it.

"And at the same time," Jim went on, "I'd like you to see if . . . I mean to feel . . . whether there are any iron 'roves'.

"What are they?"

"They are diamond-shaped metal washers. They would be inside the boat on the nails that were used to hold two overlapping planks tightly together.

"The nails come through the bottom of the upper plank and the top of the lower one. The 'roves' would be on the end of the nails."

"Would they have survived in the water all this time?" I queried.

"Today, they will probably only be lumps of rust, it's true. You'll find them spaced about a finger-to-thumb span apart."

"You think I'll actually find some?"

"More modern boats would have used copper, so if you do find a lump of rust, from a dating point of view it will be very good news."

Chapter 22 – Dragon's Head

We had the shield boss, the scabbard decorations from a sword, and now an axe, all from the same small site.

It seemed there could be very little doubt that we did have the timbers of a real Viking ship buried in the River Ouse.

But what sort of ship was it? Could it properly be described as a longship?

There was a view at the Aldwark Museum that it could be one that had come all the way across the North Sea.

And, as I reminded them, in George's dream it was the larger vessel that had been burned, and sank.

The Aldwark Museum people did not know how to treat those dreams. I couldn't help thinking they could not be totally discounted.

What we had already found surely gave them some credence.

"I suppose you'll not be satisfied until I bring up the dragon's head from the bow," I joked.

I quickly realised that it was wishful thinking on my part.

Our experience had proved that wooden things could survive down there.

But it was doubtful whether any such dragon's head now existed, even from one of the burial ships.

If we could find that dragon, we would indeed be famous.

Chapter 23 – Call the Fire Brigade

Because of the weight of the measuring device Bill had made, we needed help from a boat to get into position.

Once set up, it did work well.

By extending the many tubes, I was able to register the position of the planks more or less where they overlapped.

Using these measurements, and my impressions in modelling clay, Jim was able to draw a fairly accurate cross section of at least a small part of the hull.

He could not produce a drawing of the whole of the hull because we didn't have any details about the keel.

Laying the keel is the first step in the construction of any vessel.

The keel is at the bottom, underneath everything else. The rest of the structure is built up from the keel.

So the size and position of the keel were vital information for making an accurate drawing.

For one thing, they would enable us to establish which end of the ship was the bow and which was the stern.

But so far I hadn't been able to identify the keel or determine the position of it.

Therefore, I couldn't be sure exactly where, along the length of the ship, our excavation was taking place.

Progress on clearing the mud with a trowel was very slow. I began thinking how we could clear away the mud more quickly.

I had the idea of using a water jet to stir up the mud. Once the mud was removed, it would be carried away by the flow of the river.

I raised the possibility with my friend at the museum.

"Jim," I asked, "can you get the loan of

a small, portable, petrol-driven pump and hose?"

"Perhaps we should start with the Fire Brigade," he suggested.

I didn't think that was a good idea.

"Their pumps will be too powerful. They'd wash everything away.

"And remember there's the back thrust effect of a fireman's hose. Whoever is holding the nozzle has to work against the force of that.

"It's really powerful, even when used in air. I dread to think what it would be like under water."

"Yes, you're right," Jim agreed.

Then he had an idea.

"Here in York," he told me, "the Fire Brigade often have to pump out flooded buildings. They use much smaller pumps for that. I know the very man to approach."

"You'd better be thinking about a nozzle that squirts both ways," I suggested.

"I've no doubt Bill, our engineering friend, can make something on those lines."

The Fire Brigade did indeed come up with a small pump that one man could carry easily.

Bill provided the nozzle. It was angled slightly outwards so as not to be a nuisance to the operator.

We even had a visit to the fire station. They were helpful, but they reminded me very firmly that at the first signs of flood conditions, the pump would have to be returned.

That was no problem, because those same flood conditions would also put an end to our underwater work.

Chapter 24 – Testing, Testing

The nozzle was heavy, so Bill welded on two large handles. That made it easier to control, but also made it even heavier.

We ended up with a polystyrene float tethered above it to take the weight.

I hoped, when I was operating it, I might at least glimpse something through the stream of clearer water below.

When it came to testing, I chose a time when the tide was ebbing.

I stuck four bright, new two-pence pieces a little below the surface of the mud, well way from my excavation.

With the nozzle only half open there was a noticeable backward thrust. However, I didn't think it was enough to be a problem.

I held my hand over the business end. The strength of the jet felt about right.

Then to work. First I moved the nozzle around in a one-foot-square pattern over the area where the coins were. Then I raised it to get clear water over the area.

Nothing much had changed.

But, after I did it twice more, two coins showed on the surface. After two more repetitions, all four coins were showing.

Clearly, the first two coins had been lifted up as the mud was disturbed, then floated down on the falling surface of the mud.

That test proved the jet was fine for metal objects. What about lighter, possibly wooden things? How would it deal with those?

We decided the best thing was to stand the riddle on its side. We positioned it immediately downstream of the coffer-dam. There, it would catch anything that might try to float away on the stream of pumped water.

The coffer-dam was now thirty inches deep.

My next task was to find out whether the flow of pumped water would be powerful enough to lift mud up and out of the coffer-dam.

This had to work now because at a later date, the coffer-dam would be even deeper.

Having stirred up the first layer of mud, midway along the coffer-dam, I aimed my jet higher. I pointed it towards the end of the coffer-dam, in the hope that it would carry some of the mud with it.

When I next felt along the timbers, the mud covering the wood was definitely less. In places I could now easily find the overlapping edges of the planks.

I was delighted to find the predicted, evenly spaced, badly rusted roves.

'Jim will be pleased to hear that,' I thought to myself. 'Surely it is confirmation that we do have a Viking boat.'

I could also feel the rounded shaft of something rather thicker than the shaft of the axe. I could not feel either of its ends.

The only thing to do was carry on 'jetting', but which way?

Was it better to face towards the bow or the stern – not that anybody knew which was which!

Chapter 25 – Washing Away the Mud

Peter, Jack and I decided we'd have to find a better word than 'jetting'. That sounded far too powerful a process.

In the end we settled for calling it 'washing',

I continued washing downstream. I was following the shaft I had found. To my annoyance, it disappeared under the end of the coffer-dam.

In the process of my washing, some of the timbers had been completely exposed.

Next time I would bring the modelling clay and record them more accurately for Jim.

I turned to work upstream. I wondered how much of the mud would fall back in again before it reached the other end of the coffer-dam.

After a while my arms were getting tired.

It was also time to come up into water clear enough to read my air gauge.

It showed only another ten minutes working time.

I decided that time could usefully be spent with the Magnet-o-meter.

Towards the upstream end of the coffer-dam I got a loud bleep. It was right up against the side wall of the coffer-dam, two hand spans from the corner. It was in line with the shaft.

'Oh, hell!' I thought. 'Why do they always try to hide just out of my reach?'

I switched to washing, aiming below the bottom of the coffer-dam wall.

Now, it cannot be good practice to undermine the wall of a trench at an excavation on land. It would certainly be considered a crime by real archaeologists.

But this is what I was doing under water.

But before I was forced up by shortage of air, I was rewarded by feeling the wooden shaft entering rusting metal.

So far as I could tell it was another axe. It was a different type and larger than the first axe I had discovered.

But the damned thing lay firmly trapped at both ends. The shaft must be at least four feet long. So it was a really fearsome weapon.

But this time there could be no quick trophy-grabbing for me.

Chapter 26 – Get It Up In One Piece

Back at the museum, Jim was very interested in my report.

"Sounds as if you've found an eleventh century, two-handed battle axe."

I was hoping that's what it was.

"It was a truly terrible weapon in the hands of a trained man," Jim went on. "Now that it is exposed – and at risk – I would like you to try to get it up . . ."

"I'll do my best . . ."

"But in one piece, please."

That was easy to say, but might not be so easy to do.

"After that," Jim continued, "it will be time to ask you to close down the site. I'm going to ask you to remove your coffer-dam and fill in the excavation. We need to protect whatever is down there.

"We'll have to get in a much bigger professional group to carry on where you and your friends left off.

"But you will get full credit for the good work you've done so far, and you can still be involved if you want to be."

That made good sense to me. I would be glad enough to pass on the big load of responsibility.

But how to get that axe up without damaging it?

Visibility under the water was nil. There was no chance that two of us working together would be able to handle that fragile shaft without breaking it.

We had to find an alternative.

The best thing I could think of was rigid plastic guttering to support the shaft.

A flat piece of plastic would need to be fixed to one side of the guttering. This would support the blade of the axe when we lifted it clear of the river.

It was vital that that shaft should be kept wet until it could be handed over to the Aldwark Museum.

We could do that when we had the axe in our length of guttering. If we closed off both ends of the guttering, that would also hold water.

But that meant extra weight, which worried me.

And how were we going to transport it on the winding and sometimes bumpy road to York?

Back in the water again with Peter and Jack, we got back to work with the hose.

Careful, prolonged washing did free the axe head. Then we turned our attention to the shaft. Soon the whole weapon was fully exposed.

Holding my breath, I ran my fingers along its length. The shaft was still in one piece. Hooray!

We positioned the guttering. I crossed my cold fingers, and we lifted cautiously.

With one hand at the midpoint of the shaft, and another taking the weight of the blade, we settled the axe into place in the guttering.

With the blade resting against the flat piece of plastic, I tied it down and made sure it was secure.

How I wished for an adhesive tape that would stick underwater!

Chapter 27 – Fame At Last

The next challenge was get the axe to the surface safely and then deliver it to Jim.

After much debate, we decided the best way to get the axe to the Aldwark Museum was by boat. That would avoid the problems of the winding road.

Henry's friend again offered his motor boat. We anchored it above the excavation.

We raised the axe in its guttering support, using two ropes. We had to take great care that we hauled them in at the same rate.

And at last, there it was, safe on board the motorboat, wet and intact.

I heaved a great sigh of relief. I basked in the glow of my friends' congratulations.

We covered the whole thing over, to keep it

hidden from prying eyes. Then, having phoned through the news of our success to Jim, we set off to York.

We expected to be met by Jim Burton and Mr Atkinson, the Aldwark Museum curator.

Much to my surprise, they had the press and photographers with them.

I was far from pleased by this. What about the secrecy we had agreed on?

Then Jim whispered to me that an official order had just been made, protecting our site. Secrecy was no longer essential.

The papers were full of our find. Soon the television news was taking an interest, too.

We had to tell them firmly there was no way we could take the battle axe to their studio. They did, reluctantly, agree to bring their TV cameras to the musuem.

And so we, and the battle axe, had our moment of both local and national fame.

Chapter 28 – Roskilde

After all the excitement had died down, I was back at the Aldwark Museum, chatting with Jim.

"What is your long term dream for this site of ours?" I asked him.

Without hesitation he replied, "To raise the whole vessel. Then have it put on public display here in York."

"That is what I'd like, too. But there are two immediate problems that come to mind."

Jim grinned at me. "Only two?"

"Well, first of all, how to do it? And next, where does the money come from?"

Jim nodded.

"It is going to be horribly expensive to get it excavated – let alone get it up out of the river.

And when we've done that, it will have to be preserved.

"I'm pretty sure it would need a new climate-controlled display hall. That would cost a fortune."

"In that case, why not a new museum all of its own?" I suggested.

"What a great idea!" Jim declared.

"I think the site the new York Viking Ship Museum should be close beside, or even overlooking, the River Ouse itself."

"Only too true," Jim agreed. "As to raising the money, it would be the only Viking longship in this country. That ought to count for something. To be a 'first' always helps."

"I hope you're right."

"There's only one way I can see to excavate it," Jim said thoughtfully.

"What's that?"

"Do a 'Roskilde', I'd say", Jim said.

"Whatever is that?"

"Like a boat excavation they did at Roskilde, in Denmark," Jim explained.

"They built a steel coffer-dam around it. Then they pumped it dry. That made the excavation easier."

"That's a brilliant idea, Jim."

"But I don't know if we could do that here. A coffer-dam like that in the River Ouse could cause a serious obstruction to the flow of water. There could be a local opposition campaign."

"Because of the danger of flooding?"

"Yes. The good citizens of York are only too well aware of that. We'd have to consult with the River Authority."

"What other problems might there be?"

"The size of the coffer-dam. It would have to allow a three foot space, for excavation work, between the steel sides of the coffer-dam and the wood of the boat."

"You're right. That would make it a pretty big coffer-dam."

"And we would have to consider the effect

of vibration from the pile driving when the coffer-dam is being built. It could do damage, if it's too close to the submerged timbers. That's something I know nothing about."

"It looks like you'll have to go to Roskilde to talk to the folk there about how they did it."

"You've dropped a real can of worms into my lap," Jim laughed. "But what a wonderful challenge it is."

Chapter 29 – To Be Continued

Jim and I discussed some other off-the-cuff solutions.

"I can think of a way to overcome panic over possible flooding," I suggested. "We could study past records and find the driest month to do the work."

"Good idea," Jim responded. "And we could promise to do a rush job. We could work day and night if need be, to complete the excavation, get the boat out and remove the coffer-dam. It may not be good archaeology," Jim smiled "but it would be good politics."

"I've had an idea," I said. "As a temporary measure, we could widen the river. We could dig out an area the same size as the coffer-dam on the opposite bank, so the flow isn't restricted."

Jim saw what I meant straight away.

"And afterwards," he said, "we could re-use the coffer-dam to form the restored river bank. Then bulldoze the soil back in again. Actually, it wouldn't hurt if the river there was left just a little wider than it was before."

"And another thing," I added, "when the archaeologists remove the wreck itself, it will permanently improve the flow of the river."

"So, one way and another," Jim summed up, "the arguments about what we want to do are not entirely negative. But we do have to be ready for opposition."

"You'll need to get support from the local press."

"And the City Council," Jim agreed. "We need them on our side right from the start.

"I know one of our strongest arguments, that should impress them," he continued. "That is the huge tourist value to York. It would be great if we could display the first and only Viking longship in this country."

We were eventually able to protect the wreck site. The site was actually in tidal waters.

Our reports and subsequent enquiries resulted in the site being officially 'designated' under the Protection of Wrecks Act, 1973.

This prohibits any interference by intruders. Only those duly authorised as licence holders will be allowed to dive on the site. They alone will be permitted to undertake such limited excavation as may be approved from time to time.

There the matter rests, at least until those in authority make up their minds what action can, or should, be taken and by whom.

And, most importantly, where the large sums of money involved are to come from.

So, dear reader, I can only say to you, and to myself, 'to be continued . . .

Characters in the story

The narrator	A diver
George	Owner of the sword
Barbara	A psychic, consulted by George
Henry	Barbara's husband
Peter	A diver
Jack	A diver
Roger Atkinson	Curator of Aldwark Museum
James or Jim Burton	Viking specialist at the museum
Bill	Engineer who builds gadgets

The Sword and the River is an extract from a
longer story which first appeared in a book
entitled The Darkest Lake by Philip Baker

ISBN 978-0-9514694-4-6